THE
DIANE GOODE
BOOK OF
⋆ AMERICAN ⋆
FOLK TALES
& SONGS

COLLECTED BY
ANN DURELL

A Puffin Unicorn

The publisher gratefully acknowledges permission to reprint on:

pages 13–15, "The Talking Mule," reproduced by permission of the American Folklore Society *Journal of American Folklore,* Vol. 38, 1925. Not for further reproduction. Copyright © Macdonald H. Leach.

pages 35–37, "Wait Till Martin Comes" by Maria Leach, reprinted by permission of Philomel Books from *The Thing at the Foot of the Bed and Other Scary Tales* by Maria Leach. Copyright © 1959 by Maria Leach, copyright renewed © 1987 by Macdonald H. Leach. Reproduced by permission of the American Folklore Society *Journal of American Folklore,* Vol. 47, 1934. Not for further reproduction.

page 41, "Good or Bad?" reproduced by permission of the American Folklore Society *Journal of American Folklore,* Vol. 7, 1948. Not for further reproduction.

pages 43–51, "The Three Girls with the Journey-Cakes," from *Tales from the Cloud Walking Country* by Marie Campbell, Indiana University Press, 1958.

PUFFIN BOOKS
Published by the Penguin Group
Penguin Books USA Inc., 375 Hudson Street, New York, New York 10014, U.S.A.
Penguin Books Ltd, 27 Wrights Lane, London W8 5TZ, England
Penguin Books Australia Ltd, Ringwood, Victoria, Australia
Penguin Books Canada Ltd, 10 Alcorn Avenue, Toronto, Ontario, Canada M4V 3B2
Penguin Books (N.Z.) Ltd, 182-190 Wairau Road, Auckland 10, New Zealand

Penguin Books Ltd, Registered Offices: Harmondsworth, Middlesex, England

First published in the United States of America by E. P. Dutton, 1989
Published in Puffin Books, 1996

1 3 5 7 9 10 8 6 4 2

This collection copyright © E. P. Dutton, 1989
Illustrations copyright © Diane Goode, 1989

THE LIBRARY OF CONGRESS HAS CATALOGED THE DUTTON EDITION AS FOLLOWS:

The Diane Goode book of American folk tales & songs/collected by Ann Durell.—1st ed.   p.   cm.
Summary: Presents a collection of folk tales and songs from a variety of regions and ethnic groups in the United States.
ISBN 0-525-44458-0
1. Tales—United States—Juvenile literature. 2. Folk songs, English—United States—Juvenile literature.
[1. Folklore—United States. 2. Folk songs, English—United States.] I. Goode, Diane. II. Durell, Ann.
89-1097 GR105.3.D53 1989 398.2'0973—dc19 CIP AC

Puffin Books ISBN 0-14-055953-1

Printed in U.S.A.

CONTENTS

INTRODUCTION

Americans love to tell stories. They make narratives out of what happened at school today and to Uncle John sixty years ago, out of funny or frightening or sad or wonderful things that happened to them or to someone they heard about. Some are set to music and sung at parties or family gatherings or to pass the time while working or traveling. Maybe this is because Americans love *listening* to stories.

This book is a collection of tales and songs for reading, for telling, for singing. All come out of our rich oral tradition—from a variety of the regions and ethnic groups that make up this country. Wherever possible, the specific state or area and ethnic origin are given with the story, as it is interesting to know where a tale comes from, but this is not intended as a scholarly book. It is, however, based on the work done by scholars in collecting folklore, and grateful acknowledgment is given for the access to those collections provided by the New York Public Library, the New York Society Library, and the Children's Literature Center of the Library of Congress. Special thanks to Margaret Coughlin, whose unique knowledge of storytelling and folktales was an invaluable resource.

YANKEE DOODLE

VERSE

Yan - kee Doo - dle went to town A - ri - ding on a po - ny,

Stuck a fea - ther in his hat And called it mac - a - ro - ni.

CHORUS

Yan - kee Doo - dle, keep it up! Yan - kee Doo - dle dan - dy,

Mind the mu - sic and the step, And with the girls be han - dy.

After each of the following verses, repeat the chorus.

Father and I went down to camp
Along with Captain Gooding,
And there we saw the men and boys
As thick as hasty pudding.

There was Captain Washington
Upon a slapping stallion,
A-giving orders to his men;
I guess there was a million.

And there we saw a thousand men
As rich as Squire David.
And what they wasted every day,
I wish it could be sa-ved.

And there I saw a pumpkin shell
As big as Mother's basin.
And every time they touched it off,
They scampered like the nation.

DAVY CROCKETT
MEETS HIS MATCH

ne time Davy Crockett was walking home in the late afternoon, right before sunset. He hadn't done much in the way of shooting that day, and he was mighty put out.

He was passing under a tall tree near the Great Gap when he looked up and spied a fat, furry coon staring down at him. He was just about to raise his gun when the coon lifted a paw and said, "Excuse me, is your name Davy Crockett?"

"It is," said Crockett.

That coon put on the saddest face you ever saw, and he said to Davy, "Then you needn't take any more trouble. I'm coming down."

The coon climbed on down that tree just as slow and mournful as could be. He just plain considered himself shot. Davy got to thinking that such a courteous critter deserved better than being skinned, so when the coon waddled up to him, he bent down and patted the little fellow on the head.

"You're a right thoughtful fellow," Crockett said. "I won't hurt you none."

The coon didn't seem surprised at all; instead, he just started backing himself off into the woods, saying, "That's mighty kind, Mr. Crockett."

"Hey now," said Davy, "what's your hurry?"

"Well, Mr. Crockett, it's not that I doubt you. No, sir. It's just that you might change your mind."

And with that, the coon was gone. And sure enough, Davy *did* change his mind, but by the time he did, that smart coon was long gone. Even Davy laughed. That was the first—and last—coon that ever outtalked Davy Crockett.

THE TALKING MULE
BLACK AMERICAN FROM NORTH CAROLINA

nce there was a man who had a mule named Sam. The mule worked hard all week, but on Sunday the man and his wife went to church and came home and ate dinner, and the mule rested.

One Sunday the man had to go to a funeral. He told his little boy to go down to the stall and put a saddle on Sam.

So the boy went down to the stall.

"Move over, Sam," he said. Then he took the bridle off the hook.

"For gosh sake, have I got to work on Sunday?" said Sam.

The boy dropped the bridle and ran out of there fast.

"Why haven't you saddled the mule?" his father asked.

"Sam don't want to work Sundays," said the boy. "He told me so."

The man was pretty mad at the boy for telling a story like that. So he went to saddle the mule himself. He picked up the bridle where the boy had dropped it.

"Move over, Sam," he said.

"You say 'Move over, Sam,' but you don't bring me anything to eat," said the mule.

The man dropped the bridle and ran out of there fast. The little dog, who had followed him, ran too.

"I never heard a mule talk before," said the man.

"Me neither," said the little dog.

Then that man did run. He ran into the house and slammed the door.

"The mule talked," said the man.

"What!" said his wife.

"I said I never heard a mule talk before and the dog said 'me neither,' " said the man.

"Ridiculous!" said the wife.

"What's ridiculous about that?" said the cat. "Who ever heard a mule talk?"

BUFFALO GAL

VERSE

As I was walk-ing down the street, down the street, down the street, a

pret-ty lit-tle girl I chanced to meet, and we danced by the light of the moon.

CHORUS

Buf - fa - lo gal, won't you come out to - night, come out to - night, come out to - night?

Buf - fa - lo gal, won't you come out to-night, and dance by the light of the moon?

VERSE

I danced with a gal with a hole in her stock - ing and her

heel kept a-knock-ing and her toes kept a-rock-ing. I danced with a gal with a

hole in her stock-ing, and we danced by the light of the moon.

CHORUS

Buf-fa-lo gal, won't you come out to-night, come out to-night, come out to-night?

Buf-fa-lo gal, won't you come out to-night, and dance by the light of the moon?

THE KNEE-HIGH MAN

BLACK AMERICAN

The knee-high man lived by the swamp. He was always wanting to be big instead of little.

He says to himself, "I going to ask the biggest thing in this neighborhood how I can get sizable."

So he goes to see Mr. Horse. He asks him, "Mr. Horse, I come to get you to tell me how to get big like you."

Mr. Horse, he says, "You eat a whole lot of corn and then you run round and round, till you been about twenty miles, and after a while you big as me."

So the knee-high man, he did all Mr. Horse told him. And the corn make his stomach hurt, and the running make his legs hurt, and the trying make his mind hurt. And he gets littler and littler.

Then the knee-high man, he sits in his house and study how come Mr. Horse ain't helped him none. And he says to himself, "I is going to see Brer Bull."

So he goes to see Brer Bull, and he say, "Brer Bull, I come to ask you to tell me how to get big like you is."

And Brer Bull, he say, "You eat a whole lot of grass and then you bellow and bellow and first thing you know, you gets big like I is."

And the knee-high man, he done all Brer Bull told him. And the grass make his stomach hurt, and the bellowing make his neck hurt, and the thinking make his mind hurt. And he get littler and littler.

Then the knee-high man, he say to himself, "I going to ask Mr. Hoot Owl how I can get to be sizable," and he go to see Mr. Hoot Owl.

And Mr. Hoot Owl say, "What for you want to be big?" and the knee-high man say, "I wants to be big so when I gets a fight, I can whip."

And Mr. Hoot Owl say, "Anybody ever try to pick a scrap with you?"

The knee-high man, he say no. And Mr. Hoot Owl say, "Well then, you ain't got no cause to fight, and you ain't got no cause to be more sizable than you is."

The knee-high man says, "But I wants to be big so I can see a far ways."

Mr. Hoot Owl, he say, "Can't you climb a tree and see a far ways when you has climbed to the top?"

The knee-high man, he say yes.

Then Mr. Hoot Owl say, "You ain't got no cause to be bigger in the body, but you sure is got cause to be bigger in the *brain*."

SWING LOW, SWEET CHARIOT

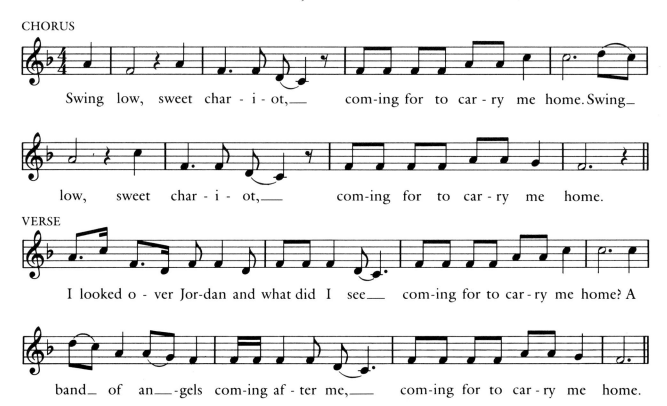

CHORUS

Swing low, sweet char - i - ot,___ com-ing for to car - ry me home. Swing___

low, sweet char - i - ot,___ com-ing for to car - ry me home.

VERSE

I looked o - ver Jor-dan and what did I see___ com-ing for to car - ry me home? A

band__ of an__-gels com-ing af - ter me,___ com-ing for to car - ry me home.

CHORUS

Swing low, sweet char - i - ot,— com-ing for to car-ry me home. Swing— low, sweet char - i - ot,— com-ing for to car-ry me home.

VERSE

If— you— get there be - fore I do,— com-ing for to car-ry me home, tell all— my friends— I'm com-ing too,— com-ing for to car-ry me home.

THE COYOTE AND THE BEAR

PUEBLO INDIAN FROM NEW MEXICO

nce upon a time, Ko-íd-deh, the bear, and Too-wháy-deh, the coyote, chanced to meet at a certain spot and sat down to talk. After a while the bear said, "Friend Coyote, do you see what good land this is here? What do you say if we farm it together, sharing our labor and the crop?"

The coyote thought well of it, and said so; and after talking, they agreed to plant potatoes in partnership.

"Now," said the bear, "I have thought of a good way to divide the crop. I will take all that grows below the ground, and you take all that grows above it. Then each can take away his share when he is ready."

The coyote agreed, and when the time came, they plowed the place with a sharp stick and planted their potatoes. All summer they worked together in the field, hoeing down the weeds with stone hoes and letting in water now and then from the irrigating ditch. When harvesttime came, the coyote went and cut off all the potato tops at the ground and carried them home. Then the bear scratched out the potatoes from the ground with his big claws and took them to his house.

When the coyote saw this, he said, "This is not fair. You have those round things which are good to eat, but what I took home we cannot eat at all, neither my wife nor I."

"But, friend Coyote," answered the bear gravely, "did we not make an agreement? Then we must stick to it."

The coyote could not answer that, but he was not satisfied.

The next spring, when they met one day, the bear said, "Come, friend Coyote, I think we ought to plant this good land again, and this time let us plant it in corn. But last year you were not satisfied with your share, so this year we will change. You take what is below the ground for your share, and I will take only what grows above."

This seemed very fair to the coyote, and he agreed. They plowed and planted and tended the corn; and when it came harvesttime the bear gathered all the stalks and ears and carried them home.

But when the coyote came to dig his share, he found only roots like threads, which were good for nothing. He was very much dissatisfied; but the bear reminded him of their agreement, and he could say nothing.

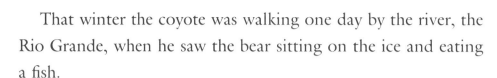

That winter the coyote was walking one day by the river, the Rio Grande, when he saw the bear sitting on the ice and eating a fish.

The coyote was very fond of fish, and he asked, "Friend Bear, where did you get such a fat fish?"

"Oh, I broke a hole in the ice," said the bear, "and fished for it. There are many here."

And he went on eating, without offering any to the coyote.

"Won't you show me how, friend?" asked the coyote, almost fainting with hunger at the smell of fish.

"Oh, yes," said the bear. "It is very easy." And he broke a hole in the ice with his paw. "Now, friend Coyote, sit down and let your tail hang in the water, and very soon you will feel a nibble. But you must not pull it out till I tell you."

So the coyote sat down with his tail in the cold water.

Soon the ice began to form around it, and he called, "Friend Bear, I feel a bite! Let me pull him out."

"No, no! Not yet!" cried the bear. "Wait till he gets a good hold, and then you will not lose him."

So the coyote waited. In a few minutes the hole was frozen solid, and his tail was stuck fast.

"Now, friend Coyote," called the bear, "I think you have him. Pull!"

The coyote pulled with all his might but could not lift his tail from the ice, and there he was—a prisoner. While he pulled and howled, the bear shouted with laughter and rolled on the ice and ha-ha'd till his sides were sore.

Then he took his fish and went home, stopping every little while to laugh at the thought of the foolish coyote.

There on the ice the coyote had to stay until a thaw liberated him, and when he got home he was very wet and cold and half-starved. And from that day to this he has never forgiven the bear, and will not even speak to him when they meet and the bear says, politely, "Good morning, friend Too-wháy-deh."

BILLY BOY

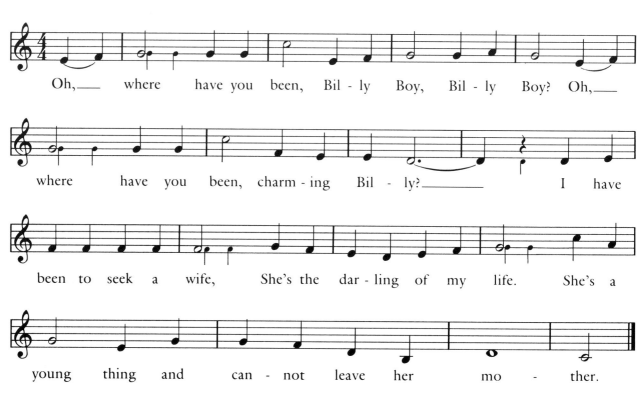

Oh,___ where have you been, Bil - ly Boy, Bil - ly Boy? Oh,___

where have you been, charm - ing Bil - ly?___ I have

been to seek a wife, She's the dar - ling of my life. She's a

young thing and can - not leave her mo - ther.

Did she bid you to come in, Billy Boy, Billy Boy?
Did she bid you to come in, charming Billy?
Yes, she bade me to come in,
There's a dimple on her chin.
She's a young thing and cannot leave her mother.

Can she bake a cherry pie, Billy Boy, Billy Boy?
Can she bake a cherry pie, charming Billy?
She can bake a cherry pie
In the twinkling of an eye.
She's a young thing and cannot leave her mother.

How old is she, Billy Boy, Billy Boy?
How old is she, charming Billy?
She's three times six, four times seven,
Twenty-eight and eleven.
She's a young thing and cannot leave her mother.

WAIT TILL MARTIN COMES

That big house down the road was haunted. Nobody could live in it.

The door was never locked, but nobody ever went in. Nobody would even spend a night in it. Several people had tried, but they came running out pretty fast.

One night a man was going along that road on his way home. Suddenly the wind came up, and the sky went black. The moon and stars disappeared. A big storm was coming fast, and he had a long way to go. He knew he couldn't get home before it broke.

So he decided to take shelter in the haunted house. *He* didn't believe in ghosts!

So in he went. He built himself a nice fire on the big hearth, pulled up a chair, and sat down to read a book.

He could hear the rain beating on the windows. Lightning flashed. Thunder cracked around the old building.

But he sat there reading.

Next time he looked up there was a little gray cat sitting by the hearth.

That was all right, he thought. Cozy.

He went on reading. The rain went on raining.

Pretty soon he heard the door creak, and a big black cat came sauntering in.

The first cat looked up.

"What we goin' to do with him?"

"Wait till Martin comes," said the other.

The man went right on reading.

Pretty soon he heard the door creak, and another great big black cat—as big as a dog—came in.

"What we goin' to do with him?" said the first cat.

"Wait till Martin comes."

The man was awful scared by this time, but he kept looking at his book, pretending to be reading.

Pretty soon he heard the door creak, and a great big black cat—as big as a calf—came in.

He stared at the man. "Shall we do it now?" it said.

"Wait till Martin comes," said the others.

That man just leaped out of that chair and out the window. When he hit the road, he was already running.

"Tell Martin I couldn't wait!" he called over his shoulder.

CLEMENTINE

VERSE

In a cav-ern in a can-yon, Ex-ca-va-ting for a mine, Lived a

mi - ner, for-ty - ni - ner, And his daugh-ter, Cle - men - tine.

CHORUS

Oh my dar - ling, oh my dar - ling, Oh my dar - ling, Cle-men - tine, You are

lost and gone for - ev - er, Dread-ful sor - ry, Cle - men - tine.

After each of the following verses, repeat the chorus.

Light she was and like a fairy,
And her shoes were number nine;
Herring boxes without topses,
Sandals were for Clementine.

Drove she ducklings to the water
Every morning just at nine;
Stubbed her toe upon a splinter,
Fell into the foaming brine.

Ruby lips above the water,
Blowing bubbles soft and fine.
But alas, I was no swimmer,
So I lost my Clementine.

GOOD OR BAD?

Two pilots went up in an airplane. The plane had a good motor."

"That's good."

"No, that's bad. The motor didn't work."

"Oh, that's bad."

"No, that was good. They had a parachute."

"Oh, that's good."

"No, that was bad. It didn't open."

"That's bad."

"No, that was good. There was a haystack under them."

"That's good."

"No, that was bad. There was a pitchfork in the haystack."

"That's bad."

"No, that was good. They missed the pitchfork."

"That's good."

"No, that was bad. They missed the haystack."

THE THREE GIRLS
WITH THE JOURNEY-CAKES

APPALACHIA

There was once a widow woman who could make good journey-cakes. She had three daughters. The oldest girl said one day, "I aim to go out in the wide world and seek my fortune. Could you fix me a snack to eat on the journey to wherever I aim to go to?" Her mammy baked two journey-cakes.

"You can have your rathers," she said to the oldest girl. "Will you take the biggest journey-cake with my curses or the least journey-cake with my blessings?"

"I aim to take the biggest journey-cake," said the oldest girl. And she wrapped it up in her Sunday best plaid shawl—blue and red and yellow it was—and set out on her long journey.

Whenever she sat down to eat, the birds and the other woods creatures gathered round her. They asked polite as you please would she give them a crumb, maybe two.

"No," she said, "I won't give you none. I ain't got hardly aplenty for my own self."

So she kept all her fine big journey-cake for herself, and the birds and the other woods creatures went hungry.

She traveled on till she come to a house, where she hired herself out to watch by the side of a dead man of a night, so his sister could get some sleep. Her wages were named to her—a peck of gold and a peck of silver and a bottle of liniment that would even cure a dead person.

All through the daytime she slept in a soft bed with a silk coverlet over her. When night came on, she sat down by the dead man to watch. But she went to sleep on the job, and the dead man's sister was so provoked, she hit her over the head and killed her and threw her body out in the high weeds and grass in the meadow.

Time passed by and the oldest girl didn't come home to the
widow woman's house. So the middle girl said, "I aim to go
out in the wide world to seek my fortune. Could you fix me a
snack to eat on the journey to wherever I aim to go to?" Her
mammy baked two journey-cakes.

"You can have your rathers," she said to the middle girl.
"Will you take the biggest journey-cake with my curses or the
least journey-cake with my blessings?"

"I aim to take the biggest journey-cake" was what the middle girl said she wanted. And she wrapped it up in her Sunday
best plaid shawl—all green and blue it was—and set out on her
long journey.

Whenever she sat down to eat, the birds and the other woods creatures gathered round her. They asked polite as you please would she give them a crumb, maybe two.

"No," she said, "I won't give you none. I ain't got hardly aplenty for my own self."

So she kept all her fine big journey-cake for herself, and the birds and the other woods creatures went hungry.

She traveled on till she came to the same house, where she hired herself out to watch by the side of the dead man of a night so his sister could get some sleep. Her wages were named to her—a peck of gold and a peck of silver and a bottle of liniment that would even cure a dead person.

All through the day she slept in a soft bed with a silk coverlet over her. When night came on, she sat down by the dead man to watch. But she went to sleep on the job and the dead man's sister hit her over the head and killed her and throwed her out in the high weeds and grass in the meadow, just like her older sister.

Time passed by and the middle girl didn't come home to the widow woman's house. The widow woman got worried and cried because she had lost two of her girls out in the wide world.

The least girl was gentle natured and she said, "Please, Mammy, hush up your crying, and I'll go and look for your two girls that's lost. And I'd be much obliged if you would fix me a little snack to eat along the way on my journey out in the wide world."

Her mammy baked two journey-cakes—a big one and a little bitty one with the scrapings of the dough.

"You can have your rathers," she said to the least girl. "Will you take the biggest journey-cake with my curses or the little bitty journey-cake with my blessings?"

"I wouldn't set out on no journey without your blessing," the least girl said. "And the little bitty journey-cake will be plenty big for me."

She wrapped the little bitty journey-cake in her second best old gray shawl and set out on her journey—no telling how long.

When it was time to eat, she called the birds and the other woods creatures about her before she unwrapped her journey-cake and sat down to eat. "Won't you have some?" she said and passed it around till she had no more than a crumb or two left for her own self.

Then she got up and walked on, and the birds and other woods creatures went along with her, though they kept hid in the edge of the woods and didn't show themselves on the public road with the least girl.

It turned out that she hired herself to do the same job her sisters had tried their luck with. Her wages were named to her—a peck of gold and a peck of silver and a bottle of liniment that would even cure a dead person.

All through the day she slept in a soft bed with a silk coverlet spread over her. When night come on, she sat down by the dead man to watch. The little birds—the night birds—sat outside the window and kept her awake.

After a time the dead man rose up in the bed.

"If you don't lay down and stay dead, I aim to hit you with this strap," she said. And he laid back down.

Time passed and the dead man rose up again. This time the least girl hit him with a strap and made him lay down dead.

Three times he rose up and the last time he jumped out of bed, and she took out after him.

The woods creatures that were big enough carried her on their backs fast as the wind through the woods. The little birds whirled about the dead man's head and the little woods creatures got under his feet and tripped him up, and after a time he gave up and laid down and stayed dead. And the least girl went back to his sister's house and collected her wages—a peck of gold and a peck of silver and a bottle of liniment that would cure even a dead person.

She hunted around in the high weeds and grass in the meadow till she found her sisters laying there dead. She rubbed the liniment on them till they come to life.

Then they all three went home again, and the widow woman made them welcome and they lived off the least girl's wages— all their lives, I reckon. A peck of gold and a peck of silver would last a mighty long time if a person never spent lavish.

ON TOP OF OLD SMOKEY

On top of Old Smo - key,_____ all cov - ered with snow,_____ I lost my true lov - er_____ for court - ing too slow._____ Now court - ing is plea - sure,_____ but part - ing is grief,_____ And a false - heart - ed lov -

er————— is worse than a thief.————————

A thief will just rob you and take what you have,
But a false-hearted lover will lead you to the grave.
The grave will decay you and turn you to dust.
Not one boy in a hundred a poor girl can trust.

    They'll hug you and kiss you and tell you more lies
    Than the crossties on the railroad or the stars in the skies.
    Come all you young maidens and listen to me:
    Never place your affection on a green willow tree.

        The leaves they will wither, the roots they will die.
        You'll all be forsaken and never know why.
        On top of Old Smokey, all covered with snow,
        I lost my true lover for courting too slow.

THE GREEDY WIFE

PUERTO RICO

There was once a married couple. He was thin— thin. She was fat—fat.

Now every afternoon when the husband came home for dinner, the wife would say, "I am not hungry, husband."

"How so?" he would ask.

"That so," she would answer him.

Yet, with every day that passed, she would gain another pound or so. At last the husband grew suspicious, and vowed that he would keep a close watch and see what happened while he was away.

So one day, instead of going to work, he hid under the house, bored a hole through the floor, and fixed his eye to it. He had not been long watching when his wife came to the kitchen, took a large bowl, and filled it with bread crumbs. Then she poured a jug of milk over them and added sugar and ate it all.

"What shall I eat now?" she asked. "I am still hungry."

It began to rain, and, since she could not go out to the store, she took a dozen eggs, some peppers and tomatoes, and made herself an omelet. Then she sat and ate it. She washed and dried the dishes, and then sat in her rocking chair and fell asleep. When she awoke, the rain was coming down in torrents.

"I cannot go out," she said, "and I am still hungry." So she went to the chicken coop, killed a chicken, fricasseed it with potatoes and onions, and ate it, bones, sauce, and all. Then she prepared a salad for her husband.

In the afternoon the husband went into the house.

"Why, husband," said the wife, "how is it that your clothes are so dry when you work out in the fields and it has been raining all morning?"

And the husband answered, "You see, wife, the drizzle in the field was as fine as the bread crumbs you had for breakfast, and yet I spent the time under a tree whose branches were as broad and wide as the size of the omelet you ate. Had it not been for that, I would have gotten as wet as the chicken in the rich sauce that you have just eaten."

The wife hung her head, for she knew her husband had found her out.

Since that day she never ate by herself again, but always waited for her husband to come home, and the two of them grew fat—fat.

I'VE BEEN WORKING ON THE RAILROAD

I've been work-ing on the rail-road all the live-long day,

I've been work-ing on the rail-road just to pass the time a - way.

Don't you hear the whis-tle blow - ing— Rise up so ear-ly in the morn?

Don't you hear the cap-tain shout-ing, "Di - nah, blow your horn"?

Di - nah, won't you blow, Di - nah, won't you blow, Di - nah, won't you blow your

horn?_____ Di - nah, won't you blow, Di - nah, won't you blow,

Di - nah, won't you blow your horn? Some-one's in the kit - chen with

Di - nah, some-one's in the kit - chen I know,_____

some-one's in the kit - chen with Di - nah, strum-ming on the old ban-

jo. He's strum-ming: Fee - fi fid-dlee - i - o, fee - fi fid-dlee - i - o,_____

fee - fi fid-dlee - i - o! Strum-ming on the old ban - jo.

THE TWIST-MOUTH FAMILY

NEW ENGLAND

Once there was a father and mother and several children, and all but one of them had their mouths twisted out of shape. The one whose mouth was not twisted was a son named John.

When John got to be a young man, he was sent to college, and on the day he came home for his first vacation the family sat up late in the evening to hear him tell of all he had learned. But finally they prepared to go to bed, and the mother said, "Father, will you blow out the light?"

"Yes, I will," was his reply.

"Well, I wish you would," said she.

"Well, I will," he said.

So he blew, but his mouth was twisted and he blew upward—this way—and he couldn't blow out the light.

Then he said, "Mother, will
you blow out the light?"

"Yes, I will," was her reply.

"Well, I wish you would," said he.

"Well, I will," she said.

So she blew, but her mouth
was twisted and she blew
downward—this way—and she
couldn't blow out the light.

Then she spoke to her
daughter and said, "Mary, will
you blow out the light?"

"Yes, I will," was Mary's reply.

"Well, I wish you would," said her mother.

"Well, I will," Mary said.

So Mary blew, but her mouth was twisted and she blew out
of the right corner of her mouth—this way—and she couldn't
blow out the light.

Then Mary spoke to one of her brothers and said, "Dick, will you blow out the light?"

"Yes, I will," was Dick's reply.

"Well, I wish you would," said Mary.

"Well, I will," Dick said.

So Dick blew, but his mouth was twisted and he blew out of the left corner of his mouth— this way—and he couldn't blow out the light.

Then Dick said, "John, will you blow out the light?"

"Yes, I will," was John's reply.

"Well, I wish you would," said Dick.

"Well, I will," John said.

So John blew, and his mouth was not twisted and he blew straight—this way—and he blew out the light.

The father said, "What a blessed thing it is to have a college education!"